Life Among The Aryans

Ishmael Reed

Published in the United States by:
Archway Editions,
a division of powerHouse Cultural Entertainment, Inc.
32 Adams Street, Brooklyn, NY 11201

www.archwayeditions.us

Daniel Power, CEO
Chris Molnar, Editorial Director
Nicodemus Nicoludis, Managing Editor
Naomi Falk, Editor

Library of Congress Control Number: 2022940430

ISBN 978-1-57687-990-0

Printed by Toppan Leefung

First edition, 2022

10 9 8 7 6 5 4 3 2 1

Edited by Naomi Falk
Photograph and scanned program courtesy Tennessee Reed
Designed by Chris Molnar

Printed and bound in China

ARCHWAY
EDITIONS

Life Among The Aryans

Ishmael Reed

Archway Editions, Brooklyn, NY

The cast from the Nuyorican Poets Café premiere production, May 31–June 24, 2018, with director Rome Neal (top row, far right).

Life Among the Aryans was originally workshopped in staged readings at the Nuyorican Poets Café in June 2017, with the support of a NYSCA grant. Directed by Rome Neal, the cast of the 2018 full production included Tom Angelo, Kim Austin, Maurice Carlton, Joseph Di Salle, Allam Forster, Eric Frazier, Jennifer Glassgow, Angela Gray, Malika Iman, Frank Martin, Lisa Pakulski, Monisha Shiva, Vernia Taylor, and Robert Turner. Set designer was Marlon Cambell; costume designer was Carolyn Adams.

Presents

Reparations Disbursement Center

DR.
2018

Ishmael Reed's
Life Among The Aryans
Directed by Rome Neal

Words From The Author

Bertolt Brecht challenged Germany's growing march toward fascism with his 1934 play, "The Mother." All that was allowed was a formal stage reading. In 2017, Ishmael Reed challenges his country's drift toward fascism with a reading of his play, "Life Among The Aryans." The time is the future. Having elected a clown president, whose administration was the worst disaster since the regime of the Romanovs, Breitbart nationalists are now confronted with the election of a Jewish president, whose FBI head is a Black man, the ultimate nightmare of Breitbart nationalism. The last straw occurs when the government decides to pay reparations to Black citizens whose ancestors suffered the horrors of slavery.

Two White nationalists, John Shaw and Michael Mulvaney, have come under the sway of an ethno-nationalist leader, the smooth talking Leader Matthews. He has persuaded his followers that a violent revolution has to occur and will take place as soon as the trucks bringing manure for the purpose of making explosives arrive. It's been a year, and his donors are getting restless.

James Baldwin never recovered from the attempt to tone down his play, "Blues For Mr. Charlie" by those whom minority writers have to please to have their plays produced. His career was damaged when he satirized these producers mercilessly in his greatest novel, "Tell Me How Long The Train's Been Gone." He accused his producers of toning down his play so that Scarsdale audiences would be comfortable. He was right. Though the Blacks loved the play, Scarsdale was offended.As a result,the producers threatened to close the show.

The attempt to stir theater away from today's vital issues demonstrates that those who tried to tone down Baldwin are still in charge. The demands of the Scarsdale audience rules The Great White Way. That's why a slave trader like Hamilton is lionized, and Andrew Jackson, a slaveholder and the Eichmann of the Native American policy is called "A Rock Star." On the other hand, Martin Luther King, Jr. is belittled by Broadway in a play that, to add to the insult, opened on the eve of his statue's unveiling.

All of my plays have been done at the Black Repertory Theater in Berkeley, California, and the Nuyorican Poets Cafe. Not once has my director, Rome Neal, or the Nuyorican attempted to shut down my message.

These are the times when, as with the Living Newspaper, a WPA theater unit of the 1930s, artists have to step in to do the job that the corporate media, which makes excuses for haters, fails to do.

The reading of this play will provide actors and actresses with an opportunity to transcend the kind of predictable and stereotypical roles offered to them by television, film and corporate theater. That has been my mission and the mission of The Nuyorican Poets Cafe.
Ishmael Reed

Life Among The Aryans
(A Stageplay)

Cast of Characters

Narrator/Newscaster: Monisha Shiva

Dobbin Robb Sobbins: N. Allam Forster

John Shaw: Frank Martin

Michael Mulvaney/Rust Belt Man: Tom Angelo

Stella Shaw: Lisa Pakulski

Jack Matthews: Timothy Mullins

Barbara Mulvaney/Reporter: Jennifer Glassgow

Dr. Krokman: Maurice Carlton

Black Man/Black John: Eric Frazier

Martha: Verinia Taylor

Stella 2: Kim Austin

Barbara 2: Angela Gray

Doris Johnson: Malika Iman

Percival Bowles: Robert Turner

Costume Designer: Carolyn Adams

Lighting Designer: Rome Neal & Malcolm Hines

Poster Graphic Design: Afiya Owens

Thank you: Michael Walker

Sound Design: Alex Santulo

Master Carpenter: Doug Wade

Set Designer: Marlon Campbell

Ishmael Scott Reed is an American poet, novelist, essayist, songwriter, editor, and publisher, who is known for his satirical works challenging American political culture.

He is a winner of the prestigious MacArthur Fellowship (genius award), the renowned L.A. Times Robert Kirsch Lifetime Achievement Award and the Lila Wallace-Reader's Digest Award. He has been nominated for a Pulitzer and finalist for two National Book Awards and is a Professor Emeritus at the University of California at Berkley.

Ishmael founded the Before Columbus Foundation, which promotes multicultural American writing. (The American Book Awards, sponsored by the foundation, has been called The American League to the National Book Awards' National League.) He also founded PEN Oakland (called "The Blue Collar PEN" by The New York Times), which issues the Josephine Miles Literary Awards.

Mr. Reed is author of thirty titles including the acclaimed novel "Mumbo Jumbo," as well as essays, plays and poetry. Titles include "The Freelance Pallbearers," "The Terrible Threes," "The Last Days Of Louisiana Red," "Yellow Back Radio Broke Down," "Reckless Eyeballing," "Flight To Canada," "Japanese By Spring" and "Juice." He is an AUDELCO and an Otto awards recipient for drama and Backstage magazine has compared him to Moliére. He is currently Distinguished Professor at The California College of the Arts.

Rome Neal (Director/ co-producer) is the Artistic Theatre Director and Chairman of the Board of Directors of the Nuyorican Poets Cafe. He received an Obie Grant with Cafe founder Miguel Algarin for excellence in theater.

He has received two Audelco Awards for directing ("Shango de Ima" by Pepe Carril and "Don't Explain" by Samuel Harp), two for acting (for the leading part in "Signs" by Gabrielle N. Lane and for Solo Performance for "Monk" by Laurence Holder) in which he also directed, and one for lighting design ("Shango de Ima" by Pepe Carril).

Neal has also the recipient of the National Black Theatre Festival's coveted Lloyd Richards Director's Award and a Monarch Merit Award for his outstanding contributions in New York Theatre. His other directing credits include "Julius Caesar Set in Africa," an adaptation of the classic play; "The Circle Unbroken is a Hard Bop" by Sekou Sundiata; "Meeting Lillie" and "Primitive World: an Anti-Nuclear Jazz Musical" by Amiri Baraka and"The C Above High C" by Ishmael Reed, all performed at the Nuyorican Poets Cafe and the National Black Theatre Festival in Winston Salem North Carolina.

Life Among The Aryans marks the 8th play of Ishmael Reed, he has directed! www.romeneal.com

Monisha Shiva: Credits include: "News from Fukushima" , "Muslim Dialogue through Mirrors Cracked", "Half Magic" , "Small Delights", "The Domestic Crusaders" , "Carroll Park ","Echoes" and "Ukkiya Jeevan." Loves socially politically conscious theater/ film. Her original acting classes are from people and their stories of struggle. A native New Yorker. Excited to be back at her old stomping ground, the Nuyorican Poet's Cafe!

N. Allam Forster is an actor, writer and Ph.D Candidate in African American Studies and Film & Media Studies at Yale University. He is currently writing a biography of the Black actor-writer-director Bill Gunn, most famous for his 1973 horror film Ganja and Hess.

Frank Martin Vietnam era US Army Veteran. Worked as a Glass Bottle manufacturing Union tradesman. Worked for and retired from IBM. Past President of a Unitarian Universalist church congregation in NC. Also sung in the churches choir. Now enjoy: Bicycling and wheel thrown pottery.

Tom Angelo is a librarian in Brooklyn who sings, writes songs and sketch comedy, and makes big plans in his free time. His presence in his Crown Heights apartment is tolerated by his cat, Mavis.

Lisa Pakulski A very concerned citizen. "Only when it is dark enough can you see the stars." Dr. Martin Luther King, Jr.

Timothy Mullins was born in Hollywood, California, served as a naval nuclear propulsion operator, obtained an engineering degree from Cal Poly, and spent some time working for the DoD. Ack. Now the stage is one of the places where his inner engineer and inner artist will hold hands and not bicker. Enjoy the show!

Jennifer Glassgow originated the role of Matchgirl in Time's Scream and Hurry on both coasts, at the Elephant Lab in LA and at the Cherry Lane in NYC. She performs with Elsinore County Theatre Company and is a member of InViolet Theatre. Television Credits include Boardwalk Empire, Criminal Minds, and the Food Network's, 24 Hour Restaurant Battle. www.jjpyle.com @aliceIW

Maurice Carlton has worked as a professional actor for more than 30 years. One of the original company members of The Billie Holiday Theater in Brooklyn, NY has won 2 Audelco Awards and nominated a total of 5 times. Most recently he produced and starred in "Uncle Tom vs. Uncle Sam", written by Bless Ji Jaja at The Symphony Space Theater in Manhattan. He looks forward to contributing to film, TV and theatrical events.

Eric Frazier (Black Man) was the solo music artist for the play "Wemmins of the Dark" at the historic Henry Street Playhouse in Soho New York City (80's) produced via auspices of Woody King Jr. He also did a tour in the New York Metropolitan area performing his own poetry for The Rennick Playwright Company . Eric is the author of Poetry books "Family, Friends and You," "Thought of a black Child" and "Black Gold and You." He has written four plays which are soon to be produced; one of which includes dance and many of his original recordings as a Jazz artist. His weekly TV show "Cultural Spectrums and Jazz Pearls Is televised 2PM Wednesdays on BRIC Arts Media TV. www.ericfraziermusic.com.

Verinia C. Taylor is a Chicago Native is a Writer/Producer Entertainer/Special Events Planner who migrated to New York City to pursue her love of writing screenplays and lyrics to showcase her talents in acting/singing and comedy. Also helped put this awesome program together. www.vctenterprises.com

Kim Austin is an accomplished actress and singer. She is currently revising her one -woman show A Sailboat to the a,musical journey of the life of Billie Holiday. She is honored to be a part of Life Among the Aryans.

Angela Gray has recently appeared in the Lynn Whitfield episode of Oprah's Master Class. She has also been trained by the Spirited Actor, Tracey Moore, who has worked with Eve, Busta Rhymes, and many more. She enjoys creating sketch comedies on her YouTube channel that include skits and karaoke videos, some which include her favorite instruments.

Malika Iman (Doris Johnson) Malika loves the arts which positively leverage political, spiritual and cultural life. Her stage credits includes working with her late father, Yusef Iman and Amiri Baraka. She is also a dancer, poet, certified Hatha Yoga instructor and author of her self-published memoirs. Malika graduated from New York University with a Bachelors in the Social Sciences and is currently a Masters candidate. She is grateful to be in this production of revolutionary theater. *"Let there be peace on earth and let it begin with me."*

Robert Turner (Percival Bowles) is one of the original members of Tshaka Ensemble (1974) and originated the role of Booker T. Washington in this production directed and written by the legendary Lou Myers who mentored him in theater. Robert is a two time AUDELCO award winner and participated in several AUDELCO nominated productions. Some of his notable roles were "Applegate" in Damn Yankees in which he won an Audelco, "Elegba" in the production of Oshun, and "Cassius" in Julius Ceasar Set in Africa in which he won an Audelco for choreography, and "Iku" in Shango de Ima directed by Rome Neal. Robert also traveled to the National Black Theatre Festival in North Carolina in several of the mentioned productions.

Marlon Campbell is a prolific Performer, Production Designer and Technical Director, working primarily in New York City he is a popular Master of Ceremonies and artist performing in venues throughout the United States and Europe. his precise, imaginative style is also applied to Digital, Video, and Graphic Design. serve as technical CCNY's Aaron Davis Hall and Sutton for the Performing Arts in Bermuda he is Executive Director for of the Living Word in Queens Chairman of the Board of Directors for the award-winning Caribbean American Repertory Theatre.

Frank Martin **Tom Angelo** **Lisa Pakulski** **Jennifer Glassgow**

N. Allam Forster **Monisha Shiva** **Robert Turner**

Maurice Carlton **Timothy Mullins** **Malika Iman**

Eric Frazier **Angela Shaw** **Kim Austin** **Verinia C. Taylor**

CONTENTS

CHARACTERS, IN ORDER OF APPEARANCE

Narrator/Newscaster: Dobbin Robb Sobbins, Pulitzer Prize winning journalist for *The New York Anglo Weekly*.

John Shaw: White male about 52 years old. Dressed in camouflage clothing, black boots.

Michael Mulvaney: White male about 23 years old. Dressed in camouflage clothing, black boots.

Stella Shaw: John's wife. White middle-aged woman. Thin. Works in a supermarket, and appears in uniform.

Barbara Mulvaney: Michael's wife. Middle-aged White woman. Works in the supermarket with her friend Stella.

Jack Matthews: Leader of a White right wing group of which John and Michael are members. Actually he is Chicago Ed, a gangster. First appears dressed in an expensive suit, wearing a flashy "diamond" ring. Should be played with W.C. Fields in mind.

Dr. Krokman: Appears to be a middle-aged Black physician or scientist, wearing a white lab coat. Actually a con artist.

Percival Bowles: Ghost of New Orleans dock worker, former member of the Screwman's Benevolent Society

Black Man: A man who has been transformed from White to Black by Dr. Krokman.

Rust Belt Man: White man who wears workers clothes but turns out not to be a worker. He is president of the local college.

Martha: Middle-aged Black woman, who is Dr. Krokman's nurse.

John 2: Black version of John Shaw, after operation.

Stella 2: Black middle-aged woman transformation of Stella 1.

Barbara 2: Black middle-aged woman actor, a transformation of Barbara 1.

Doris Johnson: Black senior woman.

ACT I, SCENE 1

NEWSWOMAN: C-Span is proud to bring you a speech by Dodd Bob Sobbins, Pulitzer Prize winner who is columnist for *The New York Anglo Weekly*. The title of the speech is "Angst In The Heartland."

DODD BOB SOBBINS: You've probably enjoyed my profound comments on government, the economy, the arts, and politics. But I'm here to confess to you that I have been wrong. How, do you ask, can a Yale graduate be wrong? I guess I am a member of the elite, out of touch with the White working class. The White working class that has been left behind, flown over, and mocked by members of the elite like me. They are disenfranchised, and turning to Opioids to soothe their depression. Instead of attending brunches in the Upper East Side, and smoking cigars at the Yale Club, I should have visited the diners, the bowling alleys and the barbershops, NASCAR, wherever they gathered, to see for myself what was happening to those who built America. Those who homeschooled instead of sending their children to schools run by the federal government. What if they believe that the world was created 6000 years ago and that people used dinosaurs for transportation. Instead of scoffing at such speculation, those of us who believe in evolution should accept this as another theory. These are people who know the Gospel by heart. Can quote it chapter and verse. They prefer buttermilk to scotch. Meat loaf to truffles. Those who were in bed by 9 p.m. after reading their children wholesome bedtime stories where the eternal moral imperatives were taught. Those who favored Country Western music over Hip Hop. But others have become so disillusioned with our institutions that they spend hours just "goofing off," watching televisions and sleeping with their babysitters. I've spent all of my time inside the Beltway where business is done on the Washington / New York shuttle. Dining in fancy French restaurants when I should have chosen Pittsburgh over Paris, Duluth over Vienna.

When we spend our time embracing identity politics, and abandoning the economic situation of the White working class, we lose. They show up at the ballot and pay us back by voting for Grade B actors and Reality show hosts. Instead of having our ear to the anxiety of real America, we tolerated all sorts of bizarre causes in the name of political correctness and multiculturalism. We refused to sympathize with the people in the Rust Belt who want to return to the world of the 1950s. As one of these members of the salt of the earth said, we want the world that we grew up in to return. Where marriage was between a man and a woman. Where Blacks dressed up in their finery to convince us that they were dignified and deserved to eat at Denny's. Where they combed their hair. Where the only concern of women was dishpan hands. Where God looked like Billy Graham.

During our debates at Georgetown dinner parties, my Conservative friends tried to warn me that the great unwashed were stirring. But now they have also been left behind. They too have been swept aside by the masses of White working class people who have had enough, who get lost in the weeds of George Wills' sentences, who take their kids to movies where none of the actors remove their clothes. They want to return to a world where you could turn on the TV without being accosted by four letter words. They're tired of carrying those who can't make the cut. Our Conservative positions and my Liberal persuasions rendered both of us blind to the problems of the forgotten Americans. Those who show up, and man up. Those who toughen up. Instead of staying holed-up in the Century Club, where one can find good conversation, a wonderful meal, and where people know how to fix a martini endowed with a kick, I plan to visit real America. I plan to find out why they became so desperate that they elected a huckster, a TV Reality show host, who posed as a populist, President P.P. Spanky, but at the inaugural ball he began turning the government over to his billionaire friends. How long will they stand being betrayed? I plan to find out by visiting a town called Whoop and Holler, Alabama. Thank you.

ACT I, SCENE 2

Two White men are seated at a table, which has three chairs.
MICHAEL *is young, about 23;* JOHN *is older, about 52. They are*
dressed in camouflage clothing. Black boots. A bottle of Jack Daniels
is on top of the table. They are drinking from glasses filled with Jack
Daniels. There are also large bags of Doritos and Taco Bell on the
table. They're listening to the radio.

NEWSWOMAN: As you know, the Clintons held all-night Bacchanals
where hooded degenerates danced around an image of Satan—
then at a pre-ordained moment, Clinton the witch would enter
carried aloft on a palanquin by four lesbians, her lovers. Clinton
is holding a sacrificial child. She placed it before a brass idol.
The idol was the image of a seated goat. Next a masked shirtless
Bill Clinton approached the altar holding a dagger. Now if you
descended to the basement you would find behind a brick wall,
Vince Foster's skeleton. You have to give the Left credit. It is an
example of their diabolical intelligence that they chose a Pizzeria
as a front for their nefarious activities—We interrupt this program, "Can Your Facts Beat Mine," for a bulletin from the
White Lightning Network: "The Zionist Occupied Government
in collaboration with their partners, the Black Panthers, and
Acorn, have decided to grant every Black man, woman, and
child reparations. $50,000.00 for their ancestors' exploitation as
slaves. If you are a Black, Reparation Disbursement Centers have
been set up where you can pick up your check. Folks, this is what
happens when the president is a Jew and the head of the FBI is a
Black woman. This has been a special bulletin from The White
Lightening Network, the voice of the Angry White Male."

JOHN *jumps up.*

MICHAEL: What the fuck!

JOHN: (*Highly agitated.*) That does it! Another giveaway. All for Black people. Nothing for White people. White people are sick and tired of this. We Whites are the real oppressed. Our brothers and sisters have nowhere to turn. Despondent, the men are given to excessive drinking and frequenting strip clubs. Leader Matthews has given us an answer to what has to be done. He says that he is only the John The Baptist of a revolution. A man will arrive on horseback, who will deliver us from the Blacks and the Muslims and the Queers and the Hispanics. We thought that President P.P. Spanky would right all the wrongs. But he packed the government with his rich friends. He spent most of his time playing golf, fending off paternity suits, and in the following election a backlash occurred. They elected this Jew president and a Black woman to head the FBI. Leader Matthews says we have been tricked again. The ballot will never work for us. It's time to assert our Second Amendment solutions. A million armed White men marching on Washington!!

MICHAEL: I hate to bring this up, John. But Matthews is hard to follow. Once again, John, where did things go wrong? What is it that we believe?

JOHN: Michael, pay attention this time. The way that Leader Matthews puts it, as far as I can follow, the 1960s were the beginning of our country's disassembling (*has difficulty pronouncing the word*). Up to then, straight, White male Protestants ran the country. Their rule had been threatened when the traitors won the Civil War, the consequences of which we are experiencing today. If the Confederacy had won the war we would have avoided the social collapse that we are experiencing. The brave leaders of the Confederacy fought to defend the Constitution, which was written by White men and for White men. Men who were not prone to political correctness. They cast inferior beings as three-fifths of a person. So for every five slaves that they had, they got three votes. These men didn't want to be overwhelmed by the popular vote cast by Northern rabble. That's why they set up the Electoral College as a bulwark against democratic fervor. The Southerners had Blacks in mind, but implicitly they meant women and other lesser folk. Of course, the Confederates got their revenge by assassinating the race traitor Abraham Lincoln, and regained their seats in Congress as a result of the enlightened leadership of President Andrew Johnson. White male rule continued until the 1950s when Martin Luther King, Jr., who was manipulated by New York Jews—as part of their plan for world domination by using the weak to overcome the strong—threatened the rule of the straight, White male Protestants. But King was taken care of. We got him out of the way, but that didn't stop the agitation, the street demonstrations, the sit-ins, the lie-ins. Women wanted their rights. The disabled, those advocating for gender reassignment. We thought that the race traitor Ronald Reagan would straighten things out, but he refused to denounce the queer Rock Hudson, his friend. We elected responsible conservatives who, instead of restoring White male rule, further eroded the country by giving in to the demands of the mud people. Those sub-human beings who were created when a volcano covered the world in darkness. Unlike White people, they lack souls, having been formed by mud. White men are still suffering from PTSD from what happened. Their wives ran away with women. Their children began listening to Rock and Roll. The only answer, according to Leader Matthews, is revolution. Deconstructing the deconstructable or something like that. Those White and Colored signs will be back up before long. Our women will be safe from a fate worse than death. There's a growing movement to end this multicultural experiment. It hasn't worked. The races should be separate. Genders should be separate. It's God's will. If George Lincoln Rockwell hadn't been killed, he would have halted the Zionist Occupation Government and its Alliance with ACORN and the Black Panther Party.

Phone rings. JOHN *picks it up.*

JOHN: O, hi David. (*Pause.*) No I told you that I don't do that anymore. Every time I think about my former trade, I get depressed. Leader Matthews convinced me that my life has a higher purpose. To restore the America that I grew up in. A place where the Dad sat comfortably in a smoking jacket, feet propped up on a stool while reading *The Saturday Evening Post*. The dog fetched your slippers. Christmas trees were green. And your spouse spent all day in the kitchen preparing a pot roast and if the kids got out of line, you smacked them one. I've stopped selling bootleg porn. (*Pause.*) There are plenty of other places where you can find combos. No. Look, I've dedicated my life to making America Great Again. Saving what remains of Western Civilization. Staving off the barbarian hordes. Standing firm against a country that is on the road to perdition. Same-sex marriage, Hip Hop, Black Lives Matter, people refusing to stand up when the Star Spangled Banner is played. Leader Matthews gave us a long list. Sorry, David. I have a new life. I have Higher goals. (*Hangs up.*)

MICHAEL: Who was that?

JOHN: David Duke. He thought that I was still peddling bootleg porno DVDs. I had to tell him that I'm a new person. No more combo porn films.

MICHAEL: I've seen him on television. He looks like a mortician does his makeup. His face is puffy. His dentures don't fit. He gets nose bleeds. The manufacturers of Botox should pay him to stay away from the tube. What on earth is combo porn? (*John whispers into Michael's ear.*) I thought that he was opposed to diversity. (*The actor playing Michael should milk this line.*)

JOHN: He made a contribution back there in the '80s, but he's over the hill now. Someone to be pitied.

Enter STELLA, JOHN'S *spouse. A thin, middle-aged White woman. She's wearing a supermarket uniform. Apron, cap. She surveys the scene. Gets huffy.*

STELLA: I have to bust my butt all day packing groceries, standing on my feet, and placing cans on shelves. I have to fend off men who want to feel me up while I take a cigarette break in the stock room and you two sit around drinking Jack Daniels and talking crap. You can at least clean up after yourselves.

STELLA *begins to remove some of the trash from the table. She begins to sweep up, angrily.*

JOHN: We're warriors, Stella. Waiting for a word from our leader to strike against the Zionist Occupied Government and their partners the Black Panthers. Leader Matthews is waiting for the manure to arrive. Then we make bombs. As soon the delivery is made, the revolution will take place. We will exercise our Second Amendment solutions. A million armed White men will march on Washington.

STELLA: It's been months. No trucks. You, Michael and other followers have given Leader Matthews money, even the jewelry that belonged to Barbara and me, and one-third of our salaries. We had to refinance our homes because he demanded it. And now we've sold most of our furniture. This table and three chairs is all that's left of the living room. Soon he will be asking us to sell our cars. Then how would I get to work? And how do you get to your whore? That Blonde, blue-eyed Viking bitch.

JOHN *rises and embraces* STELLA. *She pushes him away.*

JOHN: Stella. Sacrifices have to be made in order for our uprising to succeed. Me, Michael, and our leader Matthew are all that stands between us patriots and the arrival of black helicopters that will put us all in FEMA camps. As for Peggy, you know one of my assignments is to drill the newcomers. Guide them through the manual.

STELLA: You're drilling her all right. As for Michael here, let him make America great on his own dime. (*Pause. She sighs.*) There are some hotdogs and buns in the refrigerator. You can put them in the microwave. I don't feel like cooking for you two tonight. I'm tired. I'm going to bed. By the way, it would help if you two would get a job.

JOHN: Get a job? Who is going to hire a fifty-two-year-old White man when they can have one of these wetbacks for free?

MICHAEL: That's right. We've been left behind. Washington is spending all their time helping Queers, the disabled, Hispanics. When you go into a restroom nowadays, you don't know which form of humanity that you might encounter. And didn't you hear? They're giving reparations to Black people even though most of the slave masters were Black and the slaves were well fed and comfortable according to the White Lightening Network.

STELLA: John, you could resume your studies at that community college. Nobody told you to drop out.

JOHN: And risk coming under the sway of liberal secular Humanists? No way.

Enter LEADER MATTHEWS. *A stocky, middle-aged White man.* JOHN *and* MICHAEL *stand at attention. Give the Nazi salute.*

MATTHEWS: (*Lowers their arms. Looks around.*) We don't do that anymore. Put your hands down. No more camouflage. And easy on the Sieg Heils.

JOHN: You're just in time Leader Matthews. I was trying to tell Stella here why White men can't find work.

MATTHEWS: She doesn't know? The system is stacked against White men. Everybody knows that.

STELLA: Mr. Matthews, when are we going to have the revolution? John spends all of his time with Michael here. It's been hard. Barbara and I are becoming impatient supporting a cause when we have problems identifying what the cause is—

MATTHEWS: (*To* JOHN.) I thought you explained it to her?

JOHN: I've tried but there are some things that even I don't understand.

MICHAEL: Me too.

MATTHEWS: (*Annoyed. Sighs.*) Ok, but I hope that this is the last time that I have to explain our purpose. Please pay attention. Our enemy is radical egalitarianism which is enforced by the Zionist Occupied government. The idea that all are created equal and if some don't succeed—it's because of their early experience. It is called environmental determinism. This philosophy prevailed during the 1960s, which was the beginning of the country's decline. The proposition that the cousins of apes—the Blacks—were equal to us. That there are heritable differences in cognitive ability among the races became heresy. Those who advocated the science of this proposition were ridiculed, driven from the universities, and pie-faced in public.

This is the fundamental clash of ideas that has determined the course of human history. Whether there is an aristocracy based on possessing golden genes—comprised of those who are meant to preside over human affairs—or whether we superior beings belong on the same plane as the sub-human. Well, our position came under attack with the rise of Hitler. He went a little too far, but even he acknowledged that his ideas about genetic inferiority came from our country, where those considered inferior were sterilized and are still being sterilized, only furtively. We are people of action and shortly we will be able to use genetic editing to create the super race, the New Aryans, blonde, blue-eyed children with high I.Q.'s. They will insure the survival of the White race.

STELLA: What's going to happen to brunettes like me?

JOHN: Stella, please stop interrupting Leader Matthews and his inspiring remarks.

MATTHEWS: There are more and more people who believe as we do. With the election of a Jew who appointed a Black woman as the head of the FBI, more White people are agreeing with us. We have gone mainstream.

MICHAEL: What?

MATTHEWS: You can stop wearing those silly camouflage outfits. We're all dressing like normal people. How do you like my new suit? (*Matthews models. Michael and John nod approvingly.*)

JOHN: That's a pretty expensive suit, Leader Matthews. And what's with the diamond ring?

MATTHEWS: If I'm going to represent our organization, you wouldn't want me to dress like a bum. From now on, no more target practice in the woods, no more martial arts training. We're going to infiltrate the system by using cyberspace, hacking, Memes, Bots. Classical ways to insure a White majority. Voter suppression. We got to change our symbols. From now on we're going to call ourselves the *Die Scheiße Richtig*!! That's German.

MICHAEL, JOHN: Wow!

MATTHEWS: We have to show the opposition—the Eastern elites—that we are not ignorant bumpkins. That we're not imbeciles. That we have a theory.

MICHAEL: But I thought we were going to march on Washington.

A million armed White men. Like Hitler marched on Munich, November 8, 1923. A date that should be a national holiday. I kind of looked forward to it.

MATTHEWS: And what good did it do him? He was imprisoned. No. We're going to take over the government without firing a shot. Eliminate the responsible conservatives with insidious robo-calls. Intimidate journalists with phone and social media terror. Threaten their children. Create false news. Falsify Black-on-White crime statistics.

MICHAEL: Cyber warfare. That's expensive.

MATTHEWS: We got good news. A couple of billionaires have signed on.

JOHN: Who?

MATTHEWS: (*Hesitates. Nervously.*) They wish to remain anonymous, but they can provide us with unlimited funds. We start electing people, from the school boards to the White House. Making bombs is counterproductive. Soon our people will be installed a few doors from the Oval Office. We'll get our people on the payroll to impeach the Jew. The new president will be our puppet. We're not alone gentlemen. We have allies in Europe. Right wing parties in France, the Netherlands. In Greece, Golden Dawn has been elected to Parliament. Mussolini's party is making a comeback in Italy. We White nationalists got it going on. We're the last blue line against the invasion of Europe and America by the mud people. Blacks, Muslims, Hispanics. Our mission is to save the Judeo-Christian West. We have to remind all of the mud people that we are...are...gods.

STELLA: But I'm Irish and John is Jewish. Michael's mother was born in Scotland.

MATTHEWS: There you go, getting involved in those dreadful identity politics. The very forces against which we are opposed.

STELLA: Well now that you have some billionaires supporting the movement—the money that was spent on the trucks that were supposed to bring the manure to be used to make bombs—do we get a refund?

MATTHEWS: (*Nervously.*) Errr. They have to retrieve some money from their offshore accounts. That's going to take some time. I'm using the manure money to make repairs on our headquarters. We need a new roof.

STELLA: When do we get to see this headquarters? You keep promising to show it to us. We have the address, but you tell us to stay away.

JOHN: Stella, stop pestering Leader Matthews with so many questions. I thought that you were going to bed?

MATTHEWS: (*To Stella.*) My dear, you just have to have patience. We're making the sacrifices for you and other White women. You will be respected again. Be placed on the pedestal that you deserve. You will no longer be required to look like Kim Kardashian, the notorious race mixer. You'll be accepted as you are. Why, I happen to like small behinds. You will be treated like queens, again. Now we menfolk have some discussing to do. As for the headquarters, I'll have you come down when the do-over is completed. Surprise you.

STELLA: I should be in on this. *(Sarcastically.)* Barbara and I are footing the bills for your movement.

MATTHEWS: You will get a summary. Now run along dear.

MATTHEWS *puts his arm around Stella's shoulder and his hand slides down to her butt. She moves it away and exits.*

STELLA: Suit yourself. I'm going to take a nap.

STELLA *exits.*

MATTHEWS: John, you're going to have to do something about your woman. She doesn't seem to want to return to a time when women were regarded as sacred.

JOHN: I'll work on it. Leader Matthews, would you like a shot of Jack Daniels?

MATTHEWS *examines the refreshments lying on the table.*

MATTHEWS: Jack Daniels? Haven't you heard? The ingredients were designed by a Black man. And what are you doing with this stuff from Taco Bell and Doritos? They're an attempt on the part of Mexicans to poison White people. (*John throws the bags into the trash can*) It's called the Jalapenos' Conspiracy. Don't you listen to the White Lightening Network?

JOHN: We have it on all day.

MICHAEL: I'll never drink another drop. Why I might get contaminated.

JOHN: Me neither. I'm going to pour all of my bottles down the toilet.

MATTHEWS: By avoiding contamination, we can preserve the purity of the White race.

MICHAEL: I'm proud to be connected to such a movement. Our people in Washington must be geniuses. To think, a year ago I was selling crystal meth. Making money hand over fist. I gave up all of that for the cause.

JOHN: The cause has given me structure.

MATTHEWS: Well, I have to go. O, by the way. We need some more money. $10,000 by tomorrow noon. We need repairs for headquarters. We just had enough to cover the roof and a new foundation. But there has been a lot of water and termite damage. Some members of the volunteers say they've heard the sounds of rodents behind the walls. We will pay you back when the billionaires' checks are cleared.

MICHAEL: Barbara and Stella are getting impatient. They're doing all of the heavy financial lifting. We risk divorce by asking our wives for more money.

MATTHEWS: O, well maybe you two are not pure-blooded Aryans. Maybe you belong to the Mud People.

MICHAEL: But, Leader Matthews, Barbara and I are behind in our bills.

MATTHEWS: Sell your cars.

JOHN: How would our wives get to work? Besides, the value of my car according to Blue Book is only $1,500.

MICHAEL: My wife and I have sold most of our belongings. I don't know whether we can raise that kind of money.

JOHN: Stella is getting pretty pissed. Her salary is so small at the market. I don't know whether we can make that kind of deadline.

MATTHEWS: I thought that the blood of the super race flowed through your veins. Perhaps I was mistaken. Bring me $10,000 by tomorrow or we'll have to cast you out of the movement.

JOHN: No, please Leader Matthews. The movement has given me a purpose in life.

MICHAEL: Me too. But where are we going to find $10,000 by tomorrow?

MATTHEWS: That's your problem. I'm only following orders.

MATTHEWS *exits.* STELLA *enters.*

JOHN: Stella, where are you going?

STELLA: They just called. I have to go cover for Barbara today. She had a doctor's appointment.

MICHAEL: A doctor's appointment?

STELLA: If you'd go home from time to time, you'd find out what's happening with your wife.

MICHAEL: Go home? And deny myself the pearls of wisdom emanating from John's mouth? John is John The Baptist, Matthews is the Messiah!!

JOHN: Why thank you, Michael. Michael is a resistance fighter, Stella.

STELLA: Bullshit!

STELLA *exits.*

MICHAEL: What the hell's wrong with your wife? Doesn't she know that we're in this war to protect the purity of the White race? We're making all these sacrifices for her.

JOHN: I think that she works with some Blacks down at the market. They must have gotten to her. She was playing a Nas tape the other night.

MICHAEL: How repugnant.

JOHN: I got an idea. We can get that $10,000. Maybe $10,000 extra for me and you.

MICHAEL: I'm learning a lot hanging out with genius like you. What's the plan?

JOHN: We vowed to make any sacrifice to restore our nation to greatness. We knew that we would be tested. Now it's time to meet that challenge. Let's go. (*They exit.*)

ACT II, SCENE 1

STELLA *is alone, sitting at the table.*

STELLA: Look at all of these bills. Gas. Electric. iPhone. Groceries. Internet. Good thing I get a discount at the market. Our credit cards are maxed out. We're still paying for all of that mountain climbing gear. We gave Leader Matthews money to buy mountain climbing gear. He said that if the mud people overran Europe and the United States the only place for Whites would be the Swiss Alps. I'm beginning to think that this Matthews is full of shit. He promised me that when he and his men exercised their Second Amendment solutions that life would be better. Now after waiting for the manure to arrive, Matthews says the movement is going mainstream. Michael and John won't get jobs. Says that the revolution will start when we take our country back from the immigrants and the minorities. Why the Pakistani family living down the street is living better than we are. But, I'm beginning to have doubts. I'm beginning to think that this day will never come.

Doorbell. Stella's friend BARBARA, *Michael's wife, follows her into the room. Sits down.*

BARBARA: Where are John and Michael?

STELLA: They left here about an hour ago. I'm beginning to have doubts about Leader Matthews. First he says that we had to rent the trucks that would bring the manure with which to make bombs. Now he says that he and his followers are going to use non-violent means. That unnamed billionaires have joined the movement. But when I asked whether he was going to give us a refund, he said that he needs the money to pay the mortgage on the headquarters and make repairs. I'm beginning to have my suspicions.

BARBARA: I had the motherfucker pegged a long time ago. He asked me for some pussy.

STELLA: What? Did you tell Michael? What did he say?

BARBARA: He said I was making it up. That Leader Matthews was a man of impeccable integrity.

STELLA: He, Michael, and John must be going with each other. You can't say nothin' bad about Matthews to those two. They are hooked.

BARBARA: Michael and John and their leader, Matthews, are not going to have a revolution. I've had it with those three. I'm tired of working at the market so that Michael can come over here and drink Jack Daniels and smoke pot.

STELLA: And eat our food. One of these days, he's going to move in.

BARBARA: Don't look at me. He says that he has to hang out with John because John is his mentor.

STELLA: *(Pause.)* What did the Doctor say? Anything serious?

BARBARA: I didn't go to a medical doctor. I went to see Dr. Krokman.

STELLA: Dr. Krokman? Who is that?

BARBARA: He is the man who can turn Whites to Black.

STELLA: (*Stands up.*) What are you talking about?

BARBARA: A lot of White people are going Black. They're collecting that $50,000 reparations payment.

STELLA: But how are you—they—

BARBARA: I have to get back to the laundromat. I made an appointment with Dr. Krokman. Next time you see me, I'm going to be a Black woman. (*Barbara EXITS.*)

ACT II, SCENE 2

NEWSWOMAN: This just in. In a bold daytime holdup, two men dressed in camouflage outfits and wearing Trump masks have just robbed the First National Bank. They managed to make off with $20,000 according to bank officials. There were millions of dollars available but the two asked specifically for $20,000. We now return to our special:

Sobbins In The Rust Belt. Our correspondent Dobbin Robb Sobbins taking the pulse of real America. Their hopes and their fears.

SOBBINS: I'm now in the Rust Belt. Away from the Manhattan rat race. Why this morning in the Comfort Inn I had Wheaties for breakfast. It was refreshing. A relief from my daily regimen of Eggs Benedict and a Bloody Mary. I don't even mind the Maxwell House instead of the Peet's latte that I'm accustomed to. The sun is the boss out here. When I walked out into the Rust Belt morning I started to sing that song from—what's the name of that musical—the song goes, "Oh what a beautiful morning, oh what a beautiful day." I've decided to find out the thinking in the Heartland. Real America. Even if it means attending a stock car race or a cock fight. I'll find out why they feel they've been neglected by the upscale snobs who look down at their values. I know because I was one of them.

RUST BELT MAN *enters.*

SOBBINS: Here comes one now—Sir, can you spare a few minutes?

RUST BELT MAN: For what?

SOBBINS: I'm a columnist, from the *New York Weekly Anglo*. I've left my posh Manhattan office to come out here in the heartland where real Americans reside. Away from the Yale Club and the aristocracy who turn up their noses—

RUST BELT MAN: Look Mr., I have to do some errands. Would you come to the point? Besides you have a lot of nerve showing your face down here. They might tolerate Yankees in Birmingham, where they serve afternoon teas in the hotels, but not in Whoop and Holler. This is where real America is located. When guys divorce their wives, they marry their guns.

SOBBINS: I assure you that unlike the other networks, we believe that there are good people on both sides. I want you to tell me about your anxieties—your fears.

RUST BELT MAN: I felt less anxious when that monkey family was no longer in the White House. The Kenyan, his prostitute First Lady and their two crackhead daughters. To imagine, his picture on the walls of embassies all over the world, a disgrace to the White people who built this country. His face should have been on the cover of food stamps. I'm also upset with these greasers coming across the borders. Raping our blondes and bringing drugs into the country. Not to mention the Muslims. This country is a Christian country and I for one will pick up a gun if they try to impose Sharia law on us God-fearing Americans. We were so mad that we elected President P.P. Spanky whose administration was so incompetent that the multicultural crowd elected a Jew in the following election, which is even worse than the Muslim who got into the White House by pretending to be an American.

SOBBINS: Does your anger against the Jewish president merely mask your frustrations about jobs going overseas and White working class men like you unable to compete with cheap labor, and the replacement of manufacturing jobs with artificial intelligence?

RUST BELT MAN: I'm doing very well.

SOBBINS: Well maybe you want to create the world of the 1950s when the social order was stable—

RUST BELT MAN: The 1950s? That's when the Africanization of the West began. White kids began moving their pelvis to The Hully Gully, The Stroll, The Mash Potato, The Calypso, The Bunny Hop, The Alligator, and other profane dances. The decade ended with Chubby Checkers and The Twist. In the 1950s Rock and Roll hit the country like a musical Atomic Bomb because of Dick Clark, the worst race traitor since Eleanor Roosevelt. No, I want to return to Jane Austen's times. A time when novels ended with women getting married and Blacks were slaves.

SOBBINS: A working man like you reading Jane Austen?

RUST BELT MAN: Working man. Where did you get that idea?

SOBBINS: Your clothes.

RUST BELT MAN: Oh, these. These are my weekend casuals. My wife sent me downtown to buy some flower seeds. I'm president of the local college.

SOBBINS: So may I ask who you're voting for?

RUST BELT MAN: I'm tired of voting. I'm following the blog of a man named Leader Matthews. He's making some good points. He says a million angry White men should march on Washington. Armed. Hell I used to hide my thoughts about Blacks, Jews, and Muslims, but Leader Matthews says it's OK to release them. It's unhealthy to hold them in. Why I've sent him about $5,000 for the purpose of continuing his good work. Things in the country are going in the wrong direction. Obviously, they want to take guns away from White men like me. And if they try to take mine, I got something for them.

(RUST BELT MAN *removes a gun. Presses it against* SOBBINS' *head.*)

Comprende?

(SOBBINS *trembles. Rust Belt Man puts the gun away.*)

RUST BELT MAN: Now if you will excuse me, I have to go.

(RUST BELT MAN *exits.* SOBBINS *faints.*)

ACT II SCENE 3

Later at the Shaws' home. JOHN *enters. Wearing a Trump mask. Removes the Trump mask.* LEADER MATTHEWS *enters.*

MATTHEWS: You got the money?

JOHN *hands over a bag.* MATTHEWS *looks through the contents.*

MATTHEWS: Wonderful. You will be rewarded when we take over from the Zionist Occupied Government and crush the Black Panthers and ACORN.

JOHN: Glad to do my part, Leader Matthews. So when do we get to see the new headquarters?

MATTHEWS: I got the invitations being printed today.

JOHN: Invitations?

MATTHEWS: We're going to have a grand opening next month. Some of the Alt Right people from Washington will be there. We're flying in some of the Le Pen people from Paris, France!!!

JOHN: You can do that?

MATTHEWS: And there will be a mystery guest. We'll have prizes and games.

JOHN: Marvelous. Who is the mystery guest?

MATTHEWS: (*Looks both ways. Whispers.*) Steve Bannon!

JOHN: Steve Bannon!

MATTHEWS: (*Puts finger on lips. Looks both ways.*) Shhhhhh. (*Whispers.*) The same. And all of those who, like you, have made sacrifices will be given medals engraved with the Prussian cross. And at the banquet we will be serving Wiener Schnitzel Mit Salad.

JOHN *begins to sob.*

MATTHEWS: What's wrong?

JOHN: I'm just so touched, Leader Matthews. To think, me and Michael are part of those heroes who are part of the selfless band that is saving Western Civilization from ruin. We're like Knights.

MATTHEWS: Teutonic Knights, Matthew, Teutonic Knights. You are part of a tradition that comes from the forests of Deutschland. Thanks for the money, John.

JOHN: It was a privilege, Sir. Anything to save our shared values.

MATTHEWS *exits with the bag. Enter* MICHAEL.

MICHAEL: Barbara's gone. Kidnapped.

JOHN: Slow down, Michael. Take your time. Now what happened?

MICHAEL: I went home to take a shower and change clothes and the door was open. Barbara's clothes were missing and so was her luggage. She must have been kidnapped. It was a good idea that we hid that extra $10,000. I didn't tell Matthews that we got more than $10,000.

JOHN: Did any of the neighborhood people see anything?

MICHAEL: They said that they saw a Black woman driving away in our car. They must have put Barbara in the trunk.

JOHN: It's the Black Panthers. They're upset with us for our efforts to make America great again. They've kidnapped your wife. Did anybody see you coming here?

MICHAEL: I come here all the time. What's the matter?

JOHN: After the great revolutionary move that we just made, we have to be careful. Kidnapping Barbara is only the beginning. They'll force her to tell them our movements.

MICHAEL: Of course, you're right. What do you think that we should do?

JOHN: We have to go underground.

MICHAEL: Good idea. But what is underground?

JOHN: We'll rent a cabin in the Catskills for a few weeks until the heat is off. Besides, wearing those Trump masks concealed our identity. Underground means that we might have to wear disguises like we did during the holdup. Maybe wear beards. Dye our hair.

MICHAEL: Gee. That was fun.

JOHN: Let me leave a note for Stella. I'll say that we went looking for
Barbara's kidnappers.

JOHN *scribbles a note. They exit.*

ACT II, SCENE 4

Phone rings. Onstage we see a Black actor, who now plays Barbara. She is talking on a smartphone. Use lighting or riser to indicate some other onstage location, separated from where John and Michael were.

STELLA: Barbara!! Where are you? How are the kidnappers treating you?

BARBARA: Kidnappers. What are you talking about?

STELLA: John left a note saying that you were kidnapped by ACORN.

BARBARA: That's nonsense. I'm on a plane that's going to Bermuda. We're about to take off.

STELLA: Bermuda. What on earth are you talking about?

BARBARA: Girl, I crossed over. I've gone transracial. I'm Black.

STELLA: You're not making sense.

BARBARA: I went to Dr. Krokman. He gave me an injection of his secret formula. I was Black within five minutes. I went down to one of those Reparations Disbursement Distribution centers and picked up my reparations check.

STELLA: This doesn't make sense. Besides, you don't sound like a Black person.

BARBARA: I don't sound like a Black person? How is a Black person supposed to sound? Boy you White people are all alike. I don't sound like a Black person. How does a Black astronaut sound? How is a Black PhD or a Black general supposed to sound? We just had a Black president. Girl you been watching too many hood movies and listening to Lil Wayne. The airline attendant has told us to turn off our phones. I got to go. I'll keep in touch.

ACT II, SCENE 5

Doctor Krokman's Office. DR. KROKMAN *is a middle-aged Black man. He is dressed in a white doctor's coat. A* WHITE MAN *who has been injected with Dr. Krokman's formula stands up from the chair. The man looks into the mirror.*

BLACK MAN: Good job doc. Not only will I pick up $50,000, but my wife will think that I've gone missing. I've been looking for an excuse to get away from my wife, who has become a nudge, and the bratty kids. With the $50,000 from reparations. I can start a new life. First thing I'm going to do is buy a one-way ticket to Detroit.

BLACK MAN *exits. Enter* MARTHA, *Dr. Krokman's assistant, a middle-aged Black woman dressed in a nurse's uniform.*

MARTHA: Dr. Krokman, we have an overflow in the waiting room and people are all down the stairs and around the block. There's a big traffic jam.

MARTHA *exits.*

KROKMAN: (*To audience.*) Boy, since this reparations bill passed, I'm making millions. Enough to buy my own private jet like those Rock Stars. Before it passed, I thought I was going to go out of business. Only a few eccentric Whites were interesting in my formula. At this rate, I can buy another mansion. Two apartments in the Dakota in Manhattan. I already have a swell home upstate on the Hudson. My interior decorator is the same one who advises Ben Carson and his wife. He charges a lot but I can afford it. I even have a heated swimming pool. Tennis court.

LEADER MATTHEWS *enters. He's wearing a fake mustache, dark glasses, hat lowered over his eyes, and raincoat. He removes his hat, his fake mustache.*

KROKMAN: Well, I'll be damned. If it isn't Chicago Ed, the biggest con east of the Rockies.

MATTHEWS: Takes one to know one. How are you doing Chub?

KROKMAN *places his hand to his lips.*

KROKMAN: Shhh. My assistant might hear you. I don't go by that name here.

KROKMAN *goes to close the door.*

MATTHEWS: Oh she doesn't know about your scam? Identity theft. I see that you've found a better racket. You robbed this formula from a Black kid studying at MIT in exchange for paying his tuition. The check bounced and he sued you.

KROKMAN: How did you find that out?

MATTHEWS: I know some of the same people that you know. He took you to court. Unaware that you'd bribed the judge with counterfeit money. The judge couldn't say anything about it because he would be acknowledging that he took a bribe. Boy I've always admired your work. I need for you to give me that black injection, the formula you stole. I found some marks and took their money. With the $50,000 I'll get from reparations, I got $500,000 for Monte Carlo. Got a fake passport.

KROKMAN: What was the game?

MATTHEWS: I told them that I was going to lead a populist uprising against ZOG and the Black Panthers. The suckers gave me their life savings. Others sent money to my blog. Crowdfunding. Told them that White men should march on Washington. I posed as leader of a revolution.

KROKMAN: You—lead a revolution? (*They both laugh.*) Chicago Ed. (*Krokman doubles over with laughter.*) You were always an original when it came to scams. How did you prepare for this one?

MATTHEWS: I just memorized some of the crazy shit that's on the internet. I told the marks that they'd have to give money to buy trucks that would haul in the manure. I convinced them that we needed the manure to make bombs. It wasn't just these Joe Slobs who sent me money, but society people, and professors.

They both laugh.

KROKMAN: They all fell for that line?

MATTHEWS: Well the one guy's wife got onto me. The bitch. She kept asking when the manure trucks were going to arrive. She and the other guy's wife, Barbara, were working overtime to contribute to the cause. The cause was me. So I told them that some invisible people in Washington had changed tactics. (*They laugh.*)

KROKMAN: Did that allay her suspicion?

MATTHEWS: I had to change the story. I told them that we didn't need the manure. The bitch asked for a refund. I told her that we needed the money to improve our headquarters. I told the two imbeciles that we needed $10,000 extra.

They laugh.

MATTHEWS: After you give me the injection I'm going to fly to Monaco. Gamble. Lie on the beach. Fuck my brains out.

MATTHEWS *sits down.* KROKMAN *begins to give him an injection.*

ACT II, SCENE 6

JOHN, *hiding behind garbage can. Looks both ways.*

JOHN: Boy have I been played. That fucking Michael. What a dope. He didn't know what underground meant. We went to the cabin. So far so good. This asshole goes to the police to find out were there new developments about the kidnapping of Barbara. He dropped his iPhone when we robbed the bank. It was like the asshole delivered himself to the law. He gave me away so that he could get a light sentence. Cops come to the cabin. I had to jump out of back window. Got out of there just in time. Went to headquarters to see if Leader Matthews would hide me. No such location. The address was that of a parking lot. Good thing I kept that $10,000 in the socks drawer at home. Been calling Stella all day. She could bring the rest to me. But maybe the police have bugged her phone. What the fuck am I going to do? I'm made to look like a fool. I don't know what I'm going to do with my life, now. What can I tell my wife? She's been awaiting the revolution. I should have listened to her. She had doubts about that Matthews. If I ever get out of this jam, I'm going to make it up to her. The detectives say that the guy has been running bunko operations in twelve states. Goes by the nickname of Chicago Ed.

Enter the GHOST OF PERCIVAL BOWLES, member of the Screwman's Benevolent Society, a turn of the 19th and 20th century trade union for longshoremen. He appears before John.

GHOST: Man when are you members of the white working class going to get wise? Stop falling for con men who make promises, take your money, and politicians like President P.P. Spanky, who tell you that you're better than Jews, Blacks, Mexicans. Why can't you White workers get hip? Align yourselves with others of similar socioeconomic condition. Matthews is only the latest crook to give us, give you the old Bamboozle.

JOHN: Who the hell are you?

GHOST: Percival Bowles of the Screwman's Benevolent Society at your service. A member of the unpaid and low paid. The ones who helped to build the railroads, the ships, picked the cotton from sun up to sun down, built the homes from the log cabins to the White House and the roads from the narrow streets to the highways. We're the ones who made America great. Every brick contains a drop of our sweat. So when you White nationalists came over here, the job was already done, yet you and your people take the credit. At one time we worked side by side, but the press and the politicians divided us. They wooed you and your kind with the false promise of superiority and what has this superiority got you? Low wages, and exploitation, while your masters live like Kings.

JOHN: Yes, but they create the jobs.

GHOST: What jobs? They ain't studying you. They take their trillion dollars and store it offshore. For them there is no difference between you and those women and children in Third World nations who have no protection against the bosses keeping them in near-slavery. Countries where child labor happens every day. The top CEOs make 300 times the wages that you and your fellow members of the White working class make. Yet you became

Reagan Democrats. Let this B-rated Hollywood actor jive you with flattery, that after you finish in the bathroom perfume rises from the toilet. Instead of joining Black workers in a common struggle you let the one percent ambush you into a feudalistic protection racket. You wouldn't have what little leftover morsels the wealthy leave to you if it were not for the Unions, men and women who fought the cops and the bosses in the streets of Chicago, Detroit, Seattle, New York, Philadelphia, and what was his first act after you dummies voted him in? His first act was to break the air traffic controllers union. In the 1950s Union membership was at thirty-five percent, now it's twelve percent. The same politicians, media and management that tried to divide us back there in 1907 are dividing you from Black and Brown workers now. In those days it was the politicians, *The New Orleans Picayune Newspaper* and others on the payroll of the shippers. They tried to divide us from our White allies by assaulting us with racial epithets. Calling Black men the sons of Ham and calling our women evil-smelling Negresses. But we held out against them. Black and White.

JOHN: Whites and Blacks working side by side—you're a liar. What self-respecting White man would take orders from a Black man?

GHOST: It happened, my brother. We negotiated with the White workers for a fifty-fifty deal. If you had foremen they had to be fifty percent White and fifty percent Black. That's why the Great Levee Strike of October 1907 was probably the greatest example of labor solidarity in the history of America.

JOHN: I never heard of such a thing.

GHOST: That's because the one percent, the media, and the schools are devoted to White supremacy. Any example of cooperation between Blacks and Whites has to be erased in order for the CEOs to maintain their power. A liberal arts curriculum is a White supremacy curriculum.

JOHN: What was the cause of the strike?

GHOST: The shippers, started it. On the other side were we Screwmen, whose job was to load and unload barges of cotton. Management demanded that the Screwmen keep up with those in Galveston, Texas, who they were told stowed 200 bales of cotton per day which turned out to be a lie, but the Screwmen in New Orleans stuck to their guns. They wouldn't budge. They insisted on loading 160 bales. On October 4, the shipping lines locked the Screwmen out. Nine thousand dock workers Black and White struck to support the Screwmen. Now the White Screwmen in Galveston were like you. Thought they were better than Blacks. The management was able to manipulate the racial hatred that the White Screwmen held toward the Black workers and so as a result both worked in a condition of near-slavery.

But we in New Orleans held firm. Management—especially that of the old wicked United Fruit Company—became furious. We refused to unload their fruit. You could smell rotten fruit all over town. Well they brought in strikebreakers but many of the scabs quit when they found out they were being used. They even brought in a vigilante group called The White League. Ignorant-ass backwater types who were all hopped up on White suprema-cy when their wives and children were in rags and hungry. Their purpose was to stop, in their words, "cunning and unscrupulous Negroes in the State, and teach the Blacks to beware of fur-ther insolence and aggression." These were poor-ass rubes who believed that the ruling class gave a rat's ass about them. But we weren't intimidated. They tried to get to our wives, who were trying to feed our children, but our wives supported us. Black women even toted food from these rich White homes where they worked. On October 11, Black and White Screwmen proposed a return to work at the rate of 160 bales per day, pending an investigation into port charges and conditions. The New Orleans mayor endorsed this proposal, but employers refused and insisted on the 200 bales per day rate. In turn, the Screwmen rejected the employers' demand and held to the 160 bale rate.

JOHN: How did the whole thing end?

GHOST: The bosses, the press and the police came up with Jim Crow. They knew that solidarity between Black, White, and now Brown workers would destroy the capitalist system and replace it with interracial worker cooperatives.

JOHN *turns his back on the* GHOST *to light a cigarette. But when* JOHN *turns around the* GHOST *has vanished.*

ACT III, SCENE 1

NEWSWOMAN: John Shaw was sentenced to twenty years in prison for his role in a bank robbery that netted him and his partner Michael Mulvaney only $20,000 when millions were available. The robbery was bungled because Mulvaney left his iPhone at the crime scene. Shaw was found hiding near a garbage can. When captured, Shaw was found babbling incoherently about having communicated with the ghost of a New Orleans longshoreman. His statement upon being sentenced was equally bizarre and incoherent.

Cut to court room.

JOHN: I plead guilty, but if I am guilty so is the First National Bank who has foreclosed on thousands of residents by using falsehoods and lies. If I am guilty, so are the insurance companies that refuse to pay up to widows and survivors. If I am guilty so is Wells Fargo Bank, which forced its underlings to open accounts with customers' names without the customers being aware. If I am found guilty, is HSBC Bank guilty for laundering drug money? If I'm guilty so are universities like Georgetown who paid their bills by selling slaves. If I am guilty so are the pharmaceutical companies who use prisoners for experiments without their knowledge. Yes, I am a member of the so-called White working class, but this member is someone who is tired of being used. Used by the politicians, the billionaires and their media, used by advertisers into buying things I didn't need. But we have been used for a few hundred years. Their telling us that we were better than Blacks and Browns became our high. More dangerous than

Opioids. We sacrificed our sons and daughters in wars which benefited their bank accounts while their sons and daughters got deferments. We tolerated their CEOs receiving hundreds of times the pay that we received. We stopped joining unions. We listened to their propaganda networks like White Lightening, because they made us feel good. Well let me tell you something. My being better than Blacks and Browns can't pay the rent, can't put food on the table, can't get my children an education.

OFF-STAGE VOICE: That's enough Mr. Shaw.

JOHN: Yes, you might put me away, but wherever you put me I'll be the new John Shaw. A man who is con-proof. Joining my fellow prisoners as we go on strike against solitary confinement, bad food, the elimination of Pell grants. And turning me loose in the prison library will be your everlasting regret.

Banging of a gavel.

OFF-STAGE VOICE: Guards get him out of my sight.

ACT III, SCENE 2

NEWSCASTER: Here is a bulletin. On the way to Sing Sing Prison where he was scheduled to start serving time, John Shaw was liberated when his van was beset by some men who were described as longshoremen. People are warned to stay indoors as a manhunt is underway.

SOBBINS: I've been searching all over Whoop and Holler for a Black person and I finally found one. Your name, Ma'm.

JOHNSON: Doris Johnson.

SOBBINS: You're all out of breath, where are you running off to?

JOHNSON: I'm trying to meet the 6 PM deadline.

SOBBINS: What deadline?

JOHNSON: All Black people have to be out of Whoop and Holler by 6 PM. This is a Sundown town.

SOBBINS: A Sundown town, what do you mean?

JOHNSON: It means that my Black behind has to be out of town by 6 PM when the sun goes down. That goes for Yankees like you too. To the people of Whoop and Holler, you're a carpetbagger and an outside agitator.

SOBBINS: (*To* AUDIENCE.) As you can see, there are Black paranoids as well as White ones. Mrs. Johnson, I have talked to some of the hard working God-fearing members of the White working class who have been left behind who believe that everything is being given to Blacks, when it is Whites who are disenfranchised—

JOHNSON: Disenfranchised? They can vote. We can't. What makes them disenfranchised?

SOBBINS: Well, they can vote, but they get betrayed by the people whom they elect. They vote for a person who promises to have their backs—next thing you know they're being bought out by Goldman Sachs.

JOHNSON: Well at least they have a choice. And where do they get the idea that everything is for Blacks? Some members of my family have lost their homes because of foreclosure and my husband and I aren't doing all that well. I come over here to do day work and receive little money in return. Sometimes I just get food or clothing in return. Everything going to Blacks? White folks in this country have been taken care of more than any folks in the history of the world. They got all the land belonging to the Indians. They got all of the Roosevelt programs first, like Social Security. They deliberately left out farmers and domestics, which were fields our people were consigned to. They got the G.I. Bill. My father fought in World War II and got nothin' but an amputated leg. They get most of the Medicare, Medicaid. They got home ownership while we were red lined. So what on earth are they bitchin' about? They the most spoiled people on earth.

SOBBINS: But now you must be gratified that the government is awarding families reparations. What are you going to do with yours?

JOHNSON: We showed up at the Reparations Disbursement Center for our checks. And were turned away.

SOBBINS: Why?

JOHNSON: They said that we had the wrong identification. Now I have to run and catch this bus. And you should be running too.

SOBBINS: Aren't you making things up? Sundown towns have to be some kind of urban myth.

JOHNSON: Suit yourself, but don't say I didn't warn you.

ACT III, SCENE 3

KROKMAN *is seen in his office. Luggage stashed in the corner.*

KROKMAN: *(On his cellphone.)* Yes, nonstop from JFK to Nice. Plus the hotel Hermitage in Monte Carlo. $9,058? That sounds right. I'd like to leave tonight. Show up two hours ahead of time? What's the weather like in Monte Carlo? First class. Aisle seat. No I don't have any dietary requests. Yes, thank you. American Express. The last four digits are 8674. Yes. Thank you.

Ends call. NURSE *enters. She notices Dr. Krokman's luggage.*

NURSE: *(Eyeing the luggage.)* Dr. Krokman, where are you off to?

KROKMAN: *(Nervously.)* Thought I'd go to the house upstate for the weekend.

NURSE: But you supposed to go up to Harvard tonight to pick up the W.E.B. DuBois medal.

KROKMAN: Tell them I'm under the weather.

NURSE: I don't blame you. It's been a hectic week. Doctor, you have one more patient.

KROKMAN: But it's after 5 p.m., I got a plane to catch, I mean, I mean I want to avoid heavy traffic in the drive up the Hudson.

NURSE: Doctor, are you alright?

KROKMAN: I'm fine nurse.

NURSE: He said that he had to hitchhike here and has been traveling all night. By the way Doctor, a detective came by today. I told him that you were busy. He started asking all kinds of questions about you. He gave me his card. Is there anything wrong?

KROKMAN: (*Nervously.*) No. Send the patient away.

NURSE: He says he has the $2,500 for the transformation.

KROKMAN: Send him in.

NURSE: I'm going home, Doctor. See you Monday.

NURSE *exiting.*

KROKMAN: Yes, of course.

JOHN *enters.*

KROKMAN: Have a seat. So you want to get in on the $50,000. I figured that if Blacks get reparations, it would be like all the other government programs. They would carry a black face, but the money would go to Whites or as Frederick Douglass said of the Freedman's Savings Bank established in 1865, that was supposed to teach the liberated slaves thrifty habits, it would be the Black man's cow, but the White man's milk, because most of the bank's loans went to Whites.

JOHN: I won't be collecting the money.

KROKMAN: (*Pauses.*) Wait a minute. Ain't you the guy who escaped from the van on the way to Sing Sing?

JOHN: You going to turn me in?

Krokman strokes his chin. Thinks.

KROKMAN: No. You have to pay me $2,500 more.

JOHN: I only had $5,000. If I pay you $2,500, that will leave nothing for me.

KROKMAN: Suit yourself.

JOHN: OK. Here. (*Hands him the money.*)

JOHN *pays* KROKMAN *the money.* JOHN *sits down.* KROKMAN *takes the needle and approaches him. They freeze.*

ACT III, SCENE 4

BLACK JOHN: (*Onstage alone, in thought.*) Maybe a change of skin will improve my shitty life. Spending all of my time worrying about what Black people are up to. What they're doing. All of the things I've missed out on. Making new friends. Taking Stella on vacation. Celebrating birthdays. I've spent years listening to White Lightening radio instead of listening to music, reading books, even going to museums. Ready to take up arms against people who are worse off than me. Waiting for manure trucks to arrive is a perfect metaphor for my life. Shit. Now that I have seen the light, I can't make it up to Stella. If I showed up at her house and she was home, she'd call the cops. I hid in the bushes so that I could see her leave for work. I wanted to get ahold of the ten thousand that I hid in a drawer. Then hitchhike to Dr. Krokman's. The house was empty and had a sold sign on the lawn. After my injection. I'll probably never see her again. If I passed her in the street she'd clutch her purse. If she saw me get on an elevator, she'd take the next one. Good thing the Longshoremen raised $5,000 for me. After the injection, I'll have $2,500 left over. Maybe I'll head West. Start a new life.

ACT III, SCENE 5

SOBBINS *runs on stage. He is disheveled. All out of breath. Tie is loose. A torn jacket.*

SOBBINS: Why I never experienced such rudeness. I had just conducted my last interview with one of the God fearing people who have been left behind, disenfranchised, and neglected by the Northeastern elite who look down upon them when a group of hooligans descended upon me. I tried to reason with them with a plea that was absolutely Jamesian in its eloquence, but that didn't persuade them. They called me a fucking Jew. My ancestors came over on the Mayflower.

They gave me a real going over. What an assault on my fragile sensibilities. All day while I was interviewing these real Americans, people were passing me notes that read 6 p.m. 6 p.m.? Doris Johnson warned me. This is a Sundown town which all Blacks and Yankees must vacate by 6 p.m. They never taught me about Sundown towns at Yale.

NEWSWOMAN: Detectives showed up at the office of Dr. Cornelius Krokman, the man who has made millions with his formula that turns White people to Black. It turns out that Dr. Krokman has been exposed as the mastermind behind a vast Identity Theft operation that robbed consumers in several states before being exposed by a student as having robbed him of the formula which the con artist used, successfully. Before entering the office they found the corpse not too far from the site. It was a Black man who had been murdered by a group calling itself The White League, which requires that every new member assassinate a Black man at random. Krokman's nurse told the officers that Krokman had gone upstate for the weekend. She said that the murdered man had been Krokman's final customer for the night.

ACT III, SCENE 6

BARBARA *and* STELLA, *played by Black actresses, are on the beach, sitting on deck chairs and drinking Pina Coladas and reading* EBONY *magazine. Reggae music in the background. Ocean sounds.*

BARBARA: Had the best night's sleep in years. None of this showing up at 6 a.m. for work.

STELLA: Me too. The room service is twenty-four hours per day. I had a shrimp cocktail at about eleven last night. Afterwards, I went for a swim.

BARBARA: My first plane ride. First class. (*They fist bump.*)

STELLA: Mine too. Wasn't that boss?

BARBARA: I'm going to get that massage today.

STELLA: I'll join you.

BARBARA: Champagne brunch tomorrow.

STELLA: I had my first Daiquiri. No more beer for me. The young men on the staff here are kind of cute. Terry McMillan was right.

BARBARA: Well maybe we can sample more than the hors d'oeuvres at the bar.

STELLA: Girl—Quit. (*They burst into laughter.*) Barbara, how do you think that we ended up with those two losers? I was young. Married John out of high school. He was voted the student most likely to succeed. He couldn't find a job and started selling crystal. But something happened when President Obama was elected. He started hanging out with an odd crowd. He went to a talk by Leader Matthews and next thing I know he was away at meetings all the time. At one of those meetings, he met Michael.

BARBARA: Michael was captain of the football team. He was recruited by the NFL and even went to a summer training session. That's where he injured his knee. He started receiving disability checks. He spent a few years hanging around the house, drinking beer and watching television. He got so crazy that he got out his old football uniform, went to a game, and limped out on the field thinking that the fans would recognize him. Nobody did. One of the security guards who tackled him and brought him to the locker room called me and told me to come get him. Then he started to go to meetings held by Leader Matthews. He cleaned himself up. He found a purpose in life and was inspired by Matthews' speeches about White men being the victims of multiculturalism and how they had to take America back block by block.

STELLA: Well, we're not thirty-five yet. This hundred thousand dollars is a start.

BARBARA: We have enough to open our own market.

STELLA: With healthy food. Fresh vegetables.

BARBARA: As soon as we finish our vacation. By the way, Stella, where'd you get that $10,000?

WAITER *comes and sets down a tray with two fresh drinks.*

STELLA: I found it in a drawer among John's socks. He's been eyeing this big old blonde who shows up at the meetings. Old bloated no-titty heifer. Guess he was going to run off with her. And here he was insisting that the only income we had was from my salary of which one-third went to the cause.

They laugh.

BARBARA: I'll drink to that.

They toast.

Curtain.